Miller: The Mostly Misunderstood Mischief-Maker Who Went Missing

Written by Rebecca Thieme-Baeseman
Illustrated by John Konecny

Published by Orange Hat Publishing 2012

ISBN 978-1-937165-32-1

www.orangehatpublishing.com

Thank you to the Ringo family,
who are the proud owners of Miller, Collins, and Hank.

To my husband, Zach, thank you for telling me to go for it!

Miller in a ring of mayonnaise
18 months old

This book belongs to:

This story is based on true people, pets, and events. The real Miller is a mischievous and loveable cat who belongs to the Ringo family. He provides the Ringos with plenty of unbelievable and memorable stories—so many, in fact, that additional books would have to be written to document them all! Miller finds himself in constant predicaments, which would make most people lose their patience, but the Ringos only find themselves even more in love with him.

Miller was a mischievous cat who was always finding some sort of trouble. He was also known to be very moody, which made his owners, the Ringos, warn any guest to avoid their mean mammal. His reputation was truly in the litter box!

Like the time he scarfed down a bunch of shredded cheese from a serving bowl right before dinner.

"But the Ringos know I prefer people food! How could I resist? Mr. Ringo shouldn't have been making tacos out in the open like that!"

Then there was the time Miller made his step-brothers, Hank and Collins, howl with fear because he had them convinced he was a jaguar lurking for prey.

"Well, let's be honest. Hank and Collins will believe anything! They are just a bunch of scaredy-cats—err . . . dogs!"

Not long after the brawl, Miller traded in his black belt for a new sport—fishing. He visited a neighbor who just put in a beautiful backyard pond filled with fancy fish. Miller must have had beginner's luck, because he managed to catch each and every one!

"What can I say? I'm a natural!"

After all of his shameful shenanigans, the neighbors had little sympathy for the Ringos when Miller was found stuck at the top of a forty-foot tree.

"My goal was simply to reach the top of the tree. It didn't occur to me how I might get back down!"

Miller was known for his antics, but his *most* memorable mischief occurred on the day he went . . . MISSING!
On that dreadful day, when the Ringos returned home from work, Mrs. Ringo asked her husband, "Have you seen Miller?"
Mr. Ringo said, "No, but I bet once I start to make dinner he'll show up." The Ringos shared an eye-roll and a giggle.

Dinner came and dinner went, but still there was no sign of Miller. Mrs. Ringo started to worry, so she and Mr. Ringo began calling for Miller. "Meow! Miller! Miiiiii . . . lllleerrrrr! Meee . . . owwww!!!"

Miller did not appear.

"Well, I wonder what sort of mischief he found tonight?" sighed Mrs. Ringo as she and Mr. Ringo crawled into bed.

Meanwhile, Miller was across the street watching as they turned out their light for an eight-hour cat nap. Then he proceeded to do what he was best at: finding some midnight mischief! Because he had missed dinner, Miller was famished. He began wandering the neighborhood in search of some good grub.

It was Miller's lucky night—garbage night! Miller was known for climbing into the cans to find leftover scraps, and tonight would be no different.

Miller climbed his way into the first can on the block. "Mmmmm, what a smorgasbord of scraps!" he exclaimed.

Suddenly, the garbage can's lid came crashing down! Miller was stuck.

Oh no! thought Miller. *How will I make my way out of this mess?* Miller tried with all his might, but he couldn't get out of that trash can. He soon became exhausted from his efforts and decided he would rest and try again later.

His cat nap lasted much longer than anticipated, and before he knew it, he was jolted awake by the sounds of the garbage truck! Miller meowed with all his might. "Meowww! Someone, anyone, please help mee . . . owww!"

Little did he know, the Ringos, dressed in their pajamas and armed with their morning coffee, were walking the neighborhood, knocking on trash cans to see if they could find him.

As the noise of the garbage truck drew nearer, Miller assumed he would be lost to the sea of trash.

Screeeeech! sounded the brakes.

The garbage can shook from the clench of the truck's robotic grip. Miller could feel the garbage can rising in the air, but suddenly it stopped, reversed, and landed back on the curb with a thud.

The lid was tossed open, and Miller was blinded by the bright morning sunlight. He felt hands reach in and pull him out.

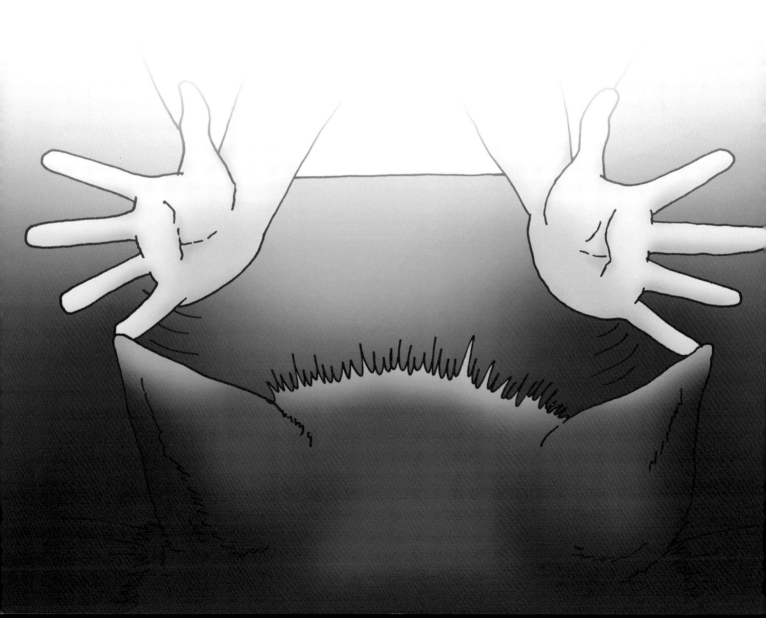

"MILLER! You bad, bad, kitty!" shouted Mrs. Ringo as she squeezed him in a smothering hug and drenched him in kisses. Mr. Ringo shook hands with the garbage collectors, thanking them for stopping the truck so they could take a peek.

"Oh, Miller, what *are* we going to do with you?" asked Mrs. Ringo.

"Well, sweetheart," said Mr. Ringo, "there's only one thing we can do."

Miller started to tense, and his fur stood straight up. *This doesn't sound good!*

CPSIA information can be obtained
at www.ICGtesting.com
Printed in the USA
LVIW010712110113
315174LV00002B